Tiger Tells All

Tiger Tells All

Ann Cameron

Illustrated by Lauren Castillo

Tamarind

TIGER TELLS ALL
A TAMARIND BOOK 978 1 848 53108 6

First published in the USA as *Spunky Tells All* by Farrar Straus Giroux
Published in Great Britain by Tamarind Books,
an imprint of Random House Children's Publishers UK
A Random House Group Company

US edition published 2011
Tamarind edition published 2013

1 3 5 7 9 10 8 6 4 2

The Random House Group Limited supports the Forest Stewardship Council (FSC®),
the leading international forest certification organization. Our books carrying the FSC
label are printed on FSC®-certified paper. FSC is the only forest certification scheme
endorsed by the leading environmental organizations, including Greenpeace. Our paper
procurement policy can be found at www.randomhouse.co.uk/environment.

Tamarind Books are published by Random House Children's Publishers UK,
61–63 Uxbridge Road, London W5 5SA

www.**tamarindbooks**.co.uk
www.**randomhousechildrens**.co.uk
www.**randomhouse**.co.uk

Addresses for companies within The Random House Group Limited can be found at:
www.randomhouse.co.uk/offices.htm

THE RANDOM HOUSE GROUP Limited Reg. No. 954009

A CIP catalogue record for this book is available from the British Library.

Printed and bound in Great Britain by CPI Group (UK), Croydon, CR0 4YY

To my dear friends Cati and Dave

Yerf!

I could tell you everything about the Bates family – things you'll never hear from anybody else. Then this book could be titled "Tiger Tells Everything". But it's not fair for a Dog to tell everything about his family. A family deserves at least some privacy and loyalty.

So I will only tell all. Almost all.

The most important thing is they love me and I love them. That's the best thing. Then there's the sad part, the sometimes tragic misunderstandings. My language is Dog. They don't understand my language.

And so they don't really understand me, even though I have lived with them for so long! Two years in Human time, which is fourteen years in Dog time. A very long time, I would say.

It's true that I can't speak Human, but I understand it – they have taught me *Sit* and *Stay*, *Come* and *Shake hands*, and *Good Dog*. Also *Bad Dog*. Besides those words, from listening carefully I have learned almost all the rest, even words they say only to each other. Although I prefer my own Dog names for some things, I know their language.

But have they learned one word in Dog? No. Have they learned any Dog customs? Very few.

Yes, they feed me, and yes, they love me. But no, they don't understand me. Only my boy, Huey, understands me. We're so close that sometimes I can read his thoughts, even though he doesn't think in Dog.

But there have been times when even Huey completely misunderstood me, as he did after I chased squirrels. (Squirrel-chasing is an ancient Dog custom I have since renounced.)

For a Dog, giving up any Dog custom is hard. Stopping squirrel-chasing was very painful for me. The day I gave it up, I grieved.

That evening, the Bates family sat around their Food Board eating hot dogs, a Human food name I don't approve of. Julian, Huey's big brother, was talking about me.

"So," he said, "there we were in the park, with Tiger going top speed after that squirrel, his legs churning up the grass, and he and the squirrel both headed straight for the river. At the last possible second, that squirrel swerved, but Tiger — he went flying over the bank and hit the river like a rock. *Kerplash!*"

"And he came out," Huey said, "looking so cold and so wet, and sooo funny!"

"Whee!" Mr Bates said, slapping his knee. "I wish I'd seen that!"

They all started chuckling about my mishap in the river. I did not appreciate it!

I sat up tall. I gave them a talk – the best talk I ever gave in my life.

I said: "Listen! I am a Dog. I will always

be a Dog, so don't laugh. You, Mr Bates, Mrs Bates, Julian and Huey, you are Humans and will always be who you are, too. Sometimes other Humans will laugh at you. That, I have noticed, is one thing Humans do: they laugh at each other.

"But a Dog will never laugh at a Human for being Human. That is why you love us. That's why you trust us. That is why you call us Man's Best Friend. Still, when we behave like Dogs because we *are* Dogs and cannot help *being* Dogs, you laugh.

"Is that fair????????????"

That was the end of my speech. I put a lot of question marks on the last word, with both my ears and my tail.

They only understood the question marks.

"Tiger's very talkative tonight," Mrs Bates said. "As if he's asking us something."

"Maybe he wants to go out," Huey said.

"Maybe he wants a bone," Julian said.

"It might have something to do with the way that squirrel humiliated him down by the river," Mr Bates said.

I didn't know that word, "humiliated". It had a terrible sound to it – the sound you would hear from a snake's tongue if it flicked you inside your nose and you couldn't stop it, or from a Human throwing a whole pan of water on your head, humidiating you for a joke.

"I was not 'humiliated'!" I told them.

Huey bent down and rubbed my neck. "Tiger's saying 'Yerf!' so much I'm afraid he'll get a sore throat."

From my whole speech, the greatest I ever made in my life, they didn't even understand the question marks. All they heard was "Yerf!"

That's how Humans are. Even a wonderful family like the Bates family.

They can't help it, and I forgive them.

My Age

The Bateses think I am a young Dog. But they don't really know. I came to them without a birth certificate or any papers whatsoever. Yes, I arrived at the Bates home as poor as a Dog can be, just looking for a place to belong.

The good thing is they don't care. I never once heard them say, "If only he'd been a Pomeranian," or "Pedigrees are better," or "You can't trust Dogs without papers." They love me for who I am. Because of that (even though I sometimes complain about them) I think they are the greatest and most wonderful family in the world, and I love them with all my heart.

But I do think about the dignity of age. The dignity of *my* age.

I am five years old. That may not seem very old to you, but, if you were a Dog, you would know the maths by heart: five Human years equals thirty-five Dog years. In Dog terms, I am thirty-five years old.

I am older than Mr Bates.

I am older than Mrs Bates.

I live in their house. They feed me. I do

what they say. Mostly. But I know very well, from what their Human adult friends call them, that they have first names. From now on I have decided to think of them as "Ralph" and "Michelle", because they are younger than I am.

That, I believe, will help me to see us as equals.

Huey Nose

Every Dog needs a boy or a girl. Huey is my boy, and I love him. I protect him. I think about him even in my dreams.

I used to believe he had a special understanding of life – that, like me, he knew the truth: the deep meaning of life comes from smells.

I overheard his silent thoughts, often the same ones: "Julian nose", "Mom nose", or "Dad nose".

I thought, My boy truly understands the world! He understands how much smell matters!

And that made me very happy. But I felt bad for him because I never once heard him say "Huey nose".

"Huey nose" is what he should have been saying most often. But he never did. I thought it was because in the Bates family, he is the youngest.

Being the youngest, he always thought everybody else had a better nose than he did, instead of realizing his nose was just fine, even if a little bit different from everyone else's. That's what I supposed.

I thought I was understanding Human as usual. Later I realized that I was mis-understanding it. Huey was really thinking: Julian *knows*, Mom *knows*, Dad *knows*. He didn't have a clue about noses!

He still doesn't. One day I will find a way to teach him.

Tiger Smells All

That's what I *really* should have called this book. Because it's true: I have an excellent nose. There has never been a smell that escaped me.

When I say I know the Bates family, I mean I *really* know them. I know their smells.

Julian smells of broccoli. That's not because he eats it. It's because he hides it in his pockets when Michelle serves it for dinner. It goes through his trouser pockets onto his skin. And there it is. Even after baths, which he takes no more often than he has to, he always has a special bitter green scent of broccoli. Humans don't notice it, but I can smell Julian coming when he's a mile away.

I can smell Huey coming from two miles away. He smells of chocolate. He likes cooking, and Michelle has taught him how to make brownies. He makes them at least twice a week. Humans can't smell Huey's chocolate smell, I guess, but I can. If he goes somewhere without me, the chocolate smell of him coming home is the smell of happiness.

Michelle smells of ginger and lemon because of certain things she cooks. I like to lick her because of that, but usually she won't let me. She says I have Dog breath.

There is nothing the matter with that! However, you have to get Humans and train them young, for them ever to appreciate Dog breath. If you don't get a Human trained early, he or she will never learn to like it. Luckily I trained Huey when he was still young, and he does like it.

Ralph smells of cars because he fixes them. Car is a very exciting smell. It reminds me of riding in my family's car and sticking my head out of the window and feeling the wind lift my ears and whirl around in my open mouth, taking my scent down the road so thousands of noses can enjoy it.

From that same fragrant wind I get knowledge of strangers I'll never meet, scents that feather their way into my nose and flutter on to my dancing brain. Smell music, that's what it's like!

One happy, fragrant afternoon Michelle and I were in the Eating Room together. She was cooking and listening to music and had a big wooden spoon in her hand. She started stirring the air in the Eating Room with big loops of the spoon until she must have had it mixed enough – because she dropped the spoon and took me by my front paws and danced with me all around the room.

"Oh, Tiger, I love this Smellody!" she said.

So of course I thought she was fully living it – the whirl of it, the swirl of it, the joyous chocolate and ginger and lemon and broc-coli and car smell she had mixed up so well.

Later, I realized she *wasn't* living it, not even partially. In fact, Michelle is mostly smell-deaf.

That day, she was only in love with sound. She doesn't even know the word "Smellody". It was an altogether different word that she was saying. She knows nothing about Smellody!

I am very sorry for Humans, really. Not only because they cannot speak Dog. Even worse: they have such big noses and yet get such little use out of them. Why? What really is the point?

You will say, Who is Tiger to question the way the universe is arranged? Who is Tiger to criticize?

I don't criticize. I don't. I just wonder. I humbly contemplate. I reflect. Sometimes I ask my departed ancestors about this, trying to reach their Sky Spirits with these questions:

Why are Humans and Dogs so different? Why are things as they are?

So far, I have received no answers.

Trouble

In spring I feel frisky, like a young pup. I want to romp. I want to play with my boy. Often he will not go outside. He won't throw a ball to me. He won't throw a stick so I can chase it. He won't stroke me. I lick him. He says, "Tiger, go away. I have homework."

What is homework? Why is homework? I do not know. For thousands of years, we Dogs have passed on to new generations the knowledge of how to survive and enjoy life. We overcame many difficult times and have populated the entire world with the great race of Dogs.

In all our many thousand years, not one of us has ever needed homework. What use is it?

Homework involves paper. Paper sport — smelling, chasing, licking, or occasionally eating paper — can be good. I know that from experience. But homework is different. Homework is doing dull things with paper.

So I reflected, one tedious spring evening, as Huey chewed on his pencil, staring at the many words he had written on a paper.

He put his chewed black pencil down by his unchewed red one. He picked up his big square rubber. (Rubbing out is a very important part of homework, probably the most important and serious part.)

But from a Dog's perspective, rubbing out, too, is very boring.

Pencil sport could be much more interesting than the way Humans play it, I thought.

That evening I asked myself: is it possible to break a pencil and make two pencils out of one?

Little in life is learned without experiment.

I reached out with my tongue and teeth and took the black pencil.

Snap! Crunch! Zlizz!

Now Huey had two black pencils instead of just one. I dropped them at his feet. I showed him that he could make even more pencils of the two I had given him. If he would only try, he could have a strong jaw, like me, and many pencils.

I picked up his red pencil. He pulled it out of my teeth. "No! Bad! Bad, Tiger! Bad Dog!"

I only wanted to teach him.

20

Maybe Huey thinks I am a bad teacher? He is wrong.

When a boy is young, it is easy to teach him the important things in life. But a Dog must teach his boy early. As our wise Dog saying goes: "You can't teach an old boy new tricks."

That is the problem. Huey is already old. If only I had raised him from puppyhood! It is no fun to be called "Bad!" for doing what is natural and right! And what Julian called me next – "Bad Bad Bad Bad!" – was even worse.

What could I do?

I left the Boy Sleeping Room, where I was not wanted. I went to the Family Lie-Around Room. Michelle was lying around in there. Newspaper was spread across her face.

If she was trying to hide, she should have used more paper. She should have covered her entire body with paper – or something more fragrant, like mud. I asked her with just a few words why she hadn't.

She said, "Aargh!" and didn't move.

I went to find Ralph.

He was in his Thinking Room. His shoes and socks were lying on the floor. He was sitting in his big lean-back chair. His eyes were shut. His legs were stretched out. His feet were high in the air. He was wiggling his toes.

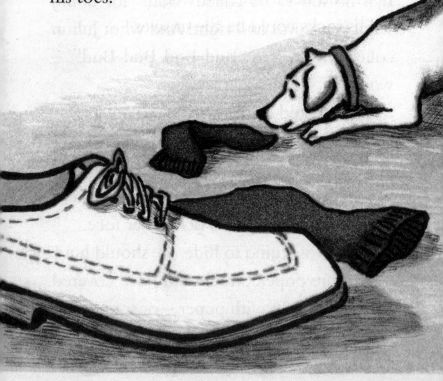

I sniffed deeply, pleasurably. Ralph had another smell besides car! An interesting smell, a delicious smell – the best smell of anyone in the Bates family. The smell was strong near his toes. But mostly, it came from his socks.

I loved Ralph. Yet he was a mystery to me.

I had always wished to know him better, but I had never found a way.

His socks could be the answer.

The Gateway

I lay on my belly and pulled myself forward, creeping towards Ralph's socks. My fur caught loudly on the rough places of the rug.

Ralph couldn't hear that sound. His ears were not good enough. This is another question I must put to the ancestors. Why do Humans have such big ears when they can hardly hear anything? What exactly is the point?

But right then I had work. I had reached the socks.

I dropped my head. I sniffed deeply. A

sweet, ripe scent filled my nostrils. I opened my jaws. The socks went into my mouth! Thousands of tiny lights in my brain flashed in spangled colours!

I sensed Ralph in a deep new way. But I couldn't concentrate on my strange knowledge. Ralph had opened his eyes.

Surely he would understand. Surely he would be happy for me.

He made strange gurgling sounds. They turned into words.

"My-y-y-y so-o-o-cks!

"Tiger! What the blazes? What the blazes has got into you?"

Nothing so far.

The socks were in my mouth, with part of one sticking out like a long black tongue. Ralph leaped out of his chair and grabbed that tongue.

"Drop 'em!" he said.

He pulled. I knew what "Drop 'em!"

meant. He wanted his socks back.

But their taste was so rich! I was learning so much!

The first of the two great Dog laws: *Smell everything and learn!*

I had to obey the second law as well. *When you get hold of something and are learning, NEVER LET GO!*

I wouldn't let go. I shouldn't let go. I was learning Ralph.

Ralph wanted me to stop learning. He very, very much wanted me to stop learning.

"Darn it, Tiger! Drop 'em!"

He pulled me into the air. I was swinging from the socks, which were swinging from his enormous hands.

We Dogs do not have homework, but we do have tests. That situation was a scary test. A test of devotion to the great Dog laws. Also, a jaw test.

My jaw is very, very good.

"Open!" Ralph roared. "Bad Dog! Open!"

I could have explained everything. But, to explain, I would have had to open. Then I would have lost the socks. Also the bright lights shining in my brain and the special knowledge I was getting. And I would have failed the test.

My jaws were clenched. Ralph lifted me high. I swung rapidly past the bookcase and the basketball trophies. I made deep sounds in my throat, talking as fast as I could:

"The nose is the gateway to life and

knowledge, Ralph. The nose takes one across the universe. With it, Dogs will one day guide Humans to the stars. Especially to the Dog star. The best place to go.

"I know how you feel, Ralph. I understand your pain. But my nose, Ralph, told me I must take your socks."

This, I sincerely believe, was my second-greatest talk ever. Delivered under difficult, nearly impossible conditions.

Ralph was swinging me in circles, round and round and round. I was dizzy. Fear had me by the stomach. Yet my brain was on fire! I was in nose paradise! I was nosing things I had never nosed before. I was understanding Ralph! Through the rich, boggy, swampy smell of Ralph's socks, his ideas, which come from the depths of the universe, bubbled up in small translucent spheres of light.

My inside self understood. The outside

me was in orbit, whirling around Ralph, rising, dropping, spinning, twisting.

I was scared, more scared than I'd ever been in my life.

Learning mattered more than fear! More than danger! I wouldn't let go!

All the coloured lights in my brain were dancing when Ralph's socks broke. I was thrown out of orbit, colliding with the wall of the Thinking Room, and sprawled out on the floor with a headache the size of the Dog star, the blazing coloured lights in my brain knocked into deep darkness.

My relatives, my ancestors, must have been proud of me. I didn't let go! And I went even beyond that.

The nose is the gateway to life and knowledge. But only the gateway. After that you have to swallow.

To this day, a few pieces of sock remain inside me. I treasure them.

The Bateses Discuss Me

I was in the doghouse. Fortunately that is only a metaphor: Ralph and Michelle don't have an actual doghouse for me. However, they left me tied up outside by the rabbit hutch all the next day.

Also they cut my Nibbles ration. They said maybe too much food was making me excitable. When night came, they let me back into the house, but they wouldn't let me sit by their Food Board. They wouldn't let me get under the Food Board and rest quietly on top of their feet. They wouldn't even let me put my head on their knees.

They made me Stay, over in my corner on my rug, by my water bowl and my empty plate, which I had licked clean and shining, while they talked about me without ever looking at me or asking me how I felt.

Ralph said, "Sometimes I think we should have got a pedigree. A dog with a more predictable character!"

It really hurt me that he would say that.

Michelle said, "You aren't too predictable yourself, Ralph! Really, you shouldn't have *swung* him."

"I was just trying to get my socks," Ralph said. "Swinging *them*. And Tiger – he just came along for the ride. It was only a few seconds."

Just a few seconds! In Dog time, it was at least five minutes. Maybe a week.

"If you had pressed on both sides of the top of his jaw, he would have had to open his mouth," Michelle said.

I wished she hadn't told Ralph a Dog secret like that. Some Dogs would bite if a person pressed their jaws open, but I would not.

"He needs to get the idea of 'Drop it!'" Julian said.

That horrible *swinging*! "Believe me, I got the idea," I told them.

They didn't understand. They talked about how I wouldn't Obey.

"Too many Nibbles are his problem," Michelle said. "They make him pigheaded."

My handsome head was reflected in my

water bowl. How could Michelle get such a silly idea? "I don't look at all like a pig. I am not a pig. I am a Dog, the best possible being to be!" I told her.

"Yerf! There he goes, getting all worked up again," Ralph said. "Treats are his problem. They make him excitable. Especially his favourite. We've got to cut it out of his diet."

I moaned. I couldn't help it, I was so sad! Hot Chilli Flavoured Tortilla Chips! My very favourite! My Saturday supper. One great joyous reason to live, and they'd take it away for ever!

And all because of socks. Just because of socks, but maybe also because of Huey's pencil, and a few other things I would just as soon not tell you about.

"Hot Chilli Flavoured Tortilla Chips! They're soooo good!" I said in Dog. I put "Please! Please! Please!" into the look in my eyes and made them turn all soft and shining. But the family – *my* family – didn't look at me. Not even Huey.

"I don't think treats or food is the problem," Julian said. "I think we're too busy. I think he needs a companion. A friend besides his bunny friends."

I beg your pardon! I thought.

The rabbits live outside in a rabbit hutch. Had it made me happy to be tied up all day near them? No!

I am an inside Dog.

When they are let out on the grass, the rabbits and I have touched noses occasionally. I am astonished by their noses. They have such small, twitchy ones. What can they nose of the universe, its depth and wonder? Not much, I don't think.

I have never tried to eat the back-yard bunnies. I admit the thought has crossed my mind. But they are my family's bunnies. I know I must not eat them. That has been clear from the first. However, they are only acquaintances, not friends. Not everybody you touch noses with is a friend. It takes more than touching noses to make a friend.

"If he had someone to play with, he would be calmer," Huey said. "Then I think he could still have Hot Chilli Flavoured Tortilla Chips."

My boy! I loved him so much! With all my heart I thanked him for understanding me and my tastes.

"*Yerf!*" Huey said. "Tiger likes the idea of having a friend!"

And Julian said, "Yes! Let's get him a cat!"

I sat up, even though they had said "Lie down!"

"Cat," I said. "Short for catastrophe. Not that. No! No cat! No, not that!"

Wild promises poured out of me.

"I won't break pencils ever again! I

won't eat any more socks! I won't chew the legs on the wicker chairs even though they smell of islands and sun and the deep salt ocean!"

I wasn't going to mention the legs on the wicker furniture, but they have slipped into this story. So be it!

"Yerf! Yerf, yerf, yerf!" Huey said, copying me. He didn't have a clue what I was saying.

"He's soooo excited," Julian said. "I guess he really wants a cat."

"I do not want a cat!!! Please, please, please! Don't get me a cat!"

But all they heard was: "Yerf!"

I sighed.

"Listen, he's sneezing," Huey said. "Maybe he's had a fever! Maybe that's the reason for everything."

"I don't think he's ill," Ralph said. "I think Julian is right. Tiger needs a cat."

"I was born with a cat allergy!" I said. It wasn't true, but I coughed so they would get the idea.

"Yes," Michelle said, "a cat. A really nice one – but one with spirit. Not the indifferent kind that lies around and doesn't want to be stroked."

A cat with spirit! What could be worse?

Still, if the only way I could get Hot Chilli Flavoured Tortilla Chips would be to share my Human family with a cat . . .

Well, I guess it could've been a whole lot worse.

Barley

We all got in the car, Ralph driving, Huey and Julian in the back, and me in the front seat, next to Michelle. I stuck my head out of the window and smelled all the swirling message-smells of the great wild blue yonder and gave my own rich smells as a gift to the world.

That is a Dog's main work. But they wouldn't let me concentrate on it. They didn't have enough understanding and respect. They had to talk to me.

"Tiger," Julian said, "guess what! We're going to let you help pick a cat!"

I didn't even pull my head back in the window. "For a barbecue?"

"Listen to that 'yerf'! He really wants a cat!" Julian said.

"For a cat barbecue," I said. "Cat with hot chilli sauce."

"He sounds as if he doesn't want a cat," Huey said.

"To me," Julian said, "it sounds as if he wants one *very much*."

"Right you both are," I said.

But all they understood was "Yerf!"

Ralph parked the car.

"Tiger," Michelle said, "here we go!" She put my lead on me, a yellow one.

We were at an Animal Shelter Hotel.

We all went in through a blue-and-red door, then down a hall, first into a room filled with big cages with Dogs in them, some hoping to be adopted and some not, and all creating many rich smells, brother

smells, sister smells, an enemy smell from a massive bulldog with a square, squashed face who the second he smelled me made a deep "Kill you!" noise in his throat and stood up on his hind legs glaring at me with eyes like burning buttons.

That was not friendly. I met his gaze sternly. I didn't wag my tail, or lower it either.

A tail is like a flag. You don't lower it before the enemy.

A woman came out of the next room. "Oh, don't worry about Barley!" she said gaily. "He doesn't mean it."

"My dear lady," I said, "I can smell him! You couldn't be more wrong!"

"Barley is a wonderful dog," the woman said, "but, so far, no one wants to take him home. Maybe you all would?"

"That canine calamity? Are you joking?" I said.

"He has the look of a fine guard dog," Ralph said.

How *could* Ralph be so ignorant? How could a good man mistake brutality for power?

"*I* am a fine guard Dog," I told him. "Maybe one day I will ask a burglar to the house, just so I can prove it. On the other hand, maybe not."

"Barley. A serious dog," Ralph said.

"What do you think, boys?" Michelle said.

Julian shrugged. Huey copied him and shrugged, too.

We Dogs don't shrug. We think it is a big mistake to be a species that shrugs. "Whatever!" is usually what a Human shrug means. A dangerous word. If you want to survive, you must pay attention to what's coming down the road straight at you and say Yes! to it, or

No! to it, but never "Whatever."

"No," I yerfed. "Ralph, Michelle – I take it back, what I said about cats. Cats and barbecues. That was nasty of me! Forget it! Yes, I used to be a carnivore! But if you get a cat, I could – I would – become a vegetarian!"

"Kill you once. Kill you twice. Kill you three times!" Barley said.

"Ralph, Michelle! I like cats so much! Cats are great! I love it that their growls are tiny and so are they. I want one! I really do!"

"Tiger, be quiet!" Michelle said. "Ralph! No second dog!"

How I adored her in that scary moment, adored her so very, very much.

Foolish

We trotted into the next room, where there were many more cages, small ones, two levels of them, and a cat in every cage, and a smell of so many different kinds of cats it made me dizzy. Tidy cats that smelled like Michelle's sewing kit, big ones almost as big as me that smelled like bears, and skinny ones that smelled of lightning and claws freshly sharpened.

When they saw me, all the cats stood up in their cages and flashed their tails back and forth like car windscreen wipers. In Dog that would have meant, "Like you a lot!" In Cat it didn't mean that at all. It meant the opposite.

I don't understand why there are so many languages in the world, and all so different.

Huey and Julian ran around to each cage, sticking their fingers through the wires and getting them cat-licked, and saying, "Cute! Cute! Cute!"

I could smell a lot of things about those cats – where they came from and what adventures they'd had, their hopes and happiness and disappointments, too.

Huey and Julian stopped to look at a small white cat who stuck one front paw out between the bars of her cage as if she wanted to shake hands with Julian.

"A friendly one!" Julian said.

He tried to touch her paw, but she pulled it back into the cage and used it to bat at the black spot on the end of her tail,

which she chased round and round until she caught it and collapsed on top of it.

I sniffed fumes of electric fur, and burning curiosity, and vanity run wild. Beyond all that, a dangerous waiting calm, like the stillness at a hurricane's centre.

"She's got energy!" Huey said.

"How cute!" Julian said.

"Don't be misled!" I said. "She'll be cataleptic, or maybe a catapult. A cat acrobat is not what you want."

"Hush, Tiger, you'll scare her!" Huey said. He and Julian kept staring at the cat and saying sweet things to her, while I sneezed and scented all the fibres of her silly fine fur. Together, what did they add up to? A very strong smell of Foolish.

I spoke to her in Dog-Cat, our limited common language. "Who are you, any-way?" I asked, figuring she might be too young or too scatter-brained to know.

She sat up, curling her tail around herself, and answered in Cat.

"I am very young. I am a pedigree. I am darling. I am dazzling. I am Balinese. I live by two mottoes: 'Better bad than bored', and 'Anything you can think of, try it!'"

"Don't just think! Reflect!" I urged.

"Zzzzush!" she said.

She had no idea what "Reflect!" meant. There was no use saying another word to her.

Through the bars in her cage, Julian and Huey took turns rubbing her neck with one finger. Huey said, "Julian, don't you think this one's the coolest?"

"Absolutely!" Julian said.

I pushed myself between them and the cage so they had to stand back a little. I tried to reason with them. I tried to warn them.

"You don't want that one. Not *her*. Never

48

take home a cat that smells of Foolish."

They ignored me.

"Mum! Dad! We like this white one best!" Julian said.

Huey said, "And see how Tiger's pushing in close! He wants her, too!"

Me and the Bates family. Together, yet we can't speak the same language. It's a tragedy.

Half an hour later they had signed the papers. They had adopted her. She was in the car, going home with us. They had already given her a name. Fiona.

Fiona sat in the back of the car in Julian and Huey's laps, tickling their chins with her tail, telling them she loved them, and distracting me from smelling anything new out of the window.

A. F.

I have never caused any trouble to the Bates family.

I am an older Dog, a considerate Dog. I always followed a daily routine.

I liked to go on walks with my family, knowing they were thinking about no one but me.

I liked my bowl with my food in it, which always sat in exactly the same place, and was just for me. I liked my water bowl, which was mine alone and sat by my food bowl.

I liked my naps. I liked my dreams. I liked

my thoughts. I liked to live in peace.

That was my old life, my life B.F. – Before Fiona.

That first day when we got home from the Animal Shelter Hotel, Fiona yowled, "Dowwwwn!"

Julian set her on the floor of the kitchen, and she ran through all the rooms of the house as fast as she could. She knocked into my food bowl and spilled the food out of it. She knocked into my water bowl and splashed all the water out. She bolted for the Family Lie-Around Room and knocked over a vase of roses and a tree of umbrellas.

"Don't chase her!" Michelle said.

We weren't chasing her. We were just trying to keep up, all saying *No!* in our own ways. A simple word.

But Fiona didn't listen. She ran into a cupboard in the Family Lie-Around Room

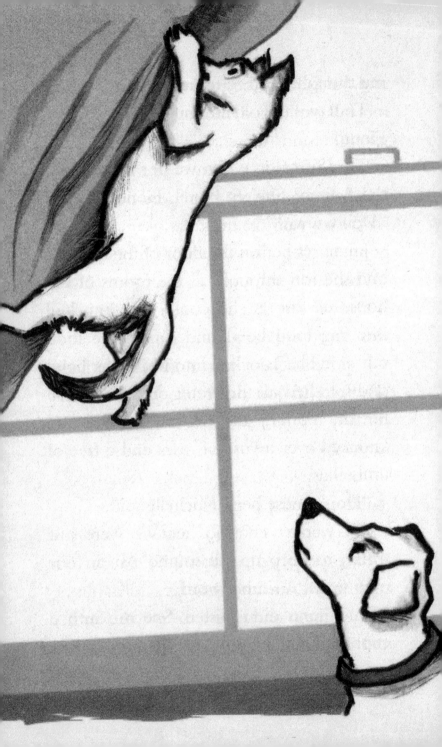

and hid behind the ironing board and the mop. Ralph tried to catch her, but just when he said "Gotcha!" the ironing board fell on his head, and she slipped out of his hands and out of the cupboard and climb-ed the curtain on the tallest window and hung by her claws, swaying and crying, "What have you done to me?"

I could see that she liked to climb but was afraid of heights.

I stood below her and said quietly, "Reflect! If you don't like heights, don't climb."

She looked down at me and hissed.

"Bring a big towel, Huey!" Ralph said. "Julian, bring the tall ladder!"

They did.

Ralph climbed the ladder. Fiona saw him coming and stretched out her claws, but he dodged them and threw the towel over her and got her all wrapped up. He climbed down the ladder one-handed, Fiona in the towel raised high above his head yowling,"I am not a package!" at the top of her lungs.

It's too bad Ralph never worked in a circus. I could see from the way he carried Fiona down that he'd have been very good at it. I thought, *Ralph, if our lives had been different, you and I could have had a circus Dog-and-Human act together, and travelled the world.*

Without Fiona, of course.

But there was Fiona twisting and trying to do somersaults inside the towel, and Ralph missing a step on the ladder, and parachuting down onto the sofa, and Fiona setting her claws into his knees through the towel, and Ralph howling, "This cat can go back where she came from!"

"Right you are!" I said, but everybody else crowded around to sit next to them on the sofa, pleading,"Oh no!"

She was not going back, no matter what Ralph and I wanted.

Julian and Huey and Michelle reached out to pat Fiona through the towel, stroking her gently for what seemed like at least a week in Dog time, until finally she let herself enjoy it and stretched out on Ralph's belly and rubbed him under his chin with the top of her white head. I waited for him to say "Down, cat!" and shove her to the floor, but he didn't. He lifted his chin higher so she could rub more, and – he purred!

Ralph purred! Just like a cat. And then Julian and Huey grinned and imitated him. They purred.

It was a terrible thing to hear, and not Human at all. I yerfed to tell Ralph and everybody how I felt, how I wouldn't be able to bear living in the Bates home if my Humans were going to start acting like cats, and Fiona raised her head and said,

"Dog, what's your problem? The way Cats act is the very best way to act!"

I yerfed again to answer her, to say — but I don't even remember now what I was going to tell her, because Michelle shushed me and told me I was being too loud, and Ralph put his hands over Fiona's ears and said, "Tiger, you must never hurt Fiona! Or scare her."

A new rule. The beginning of my life A.F. After Fiona.

Huey got off the couch and sat down on the floor and put me on his stomach and stroked me on the back and behind my ears. He was still my boy!

"Tiger's jealous," he said.

He was completely wrong about that. I was not at all jealous! It just upset me to hear a grown-up Human, my dignified friend Ralph, purring like a cat. What if he started acting like a cat all the time?

What if the rest of them did? Even Michelle? Who would fill my food bowl? Who would fill my water bowl?

The whole family would collapse. Then what?

Where would I go?

No matter. I would go! I'd take my yellow lead with me. I'd carry it in my mouth and look for a new family somewhere, a family that loved Dogs. A family without cats. A family with very severe cat allergies.

No time like the present.

My yellow lead was hanging on the doorknob. The door itself, the way to the outside, to the great wide world, hung open. All I had to do was stand up and go.

All I had to do was leave Huey. Leave Julian, Michelle and Ralph.

I could do it. I could leave them.

I could, but I couldn't. If I did, I would be a Dog with a broken heart.

Other animals, snakes for instance, or cats, can live just fine with broken hearts. They don't even notice. Hearts are not essential organs to them.

Dogs are different. We care. We can't help it. It's our nature.

Fiona was flicking her tail under Ralph's ear and purring again. Ralph was purring. Then Julian purred, and Huey, even though he still sat holding me. And Michelle, even while she stared up at the rip in the curtain – she purred, too.

If only they'd brought Barley home! We'd have had it out Dog to Dog and one of us would have lived and one of us would have died, and everything would have been simple – messy and bloody for sure, but simple, and soon over.

Life A.F. might go on for a very long time.

Fiona Rules

I thought. I reflected. I hoped: if I ignore Fiona completely, one day they will take her back where she came from.

Some very old, very patient Dogs – but probably not many – might have said my attitude was harsh. "Fiona is only a kitten, a kitten in a panic."

Not so. However, she did behave differently after she settled down.

She stopped climbing curtains after she made a bigger hole in one and fell.

She stopped hissing at me. When she saw me, she looked away. She pretended

I didn't exist.

She didn't run so much. She didn't knock into my water bowl.

No. Instead, right in front of my eyes, every day, she scooped all the water out of my water bowl with her paws, and made a puddle on the floor. Then she took my Nibbles from my food bowl, one by one, and set them in the puddle.

I liked my Nibbles crunchy! I liked them in my bowl. Not on the floor!

Since I was ignoring her completely, there was nothing I could say about this.

I vowed to continue ignoring her, to forget her presence, to be peaceful.

I couldn't get any peace taking walks with my family, though. Fiona had to go along.

I was always on my yellow lead. Fiona didn't have a lead. She ran off to smell all the smells I would have liked to smell.

On her first walk with us, we saw a man

up a ladder sawing a branch off a tree. We all wanted to keep walking, but not Fiona.

She had to butt into the branch cutting. She had to be involved. She had to get that man's attention. Fast as anything, she ran up the tree and jumped down onto the exact same branch the man was sawing off. She hung from it upside down, crying, "Help me!"

This man was a sensible person. He ignored her. Or maybe he couldn't hear her. His saw was very noisy.

She cried. He kept sawing.

She was way, way out on a limb, a big, thick branch that was being amputated and was going to land on the ground with her under it.

I watched. I tried not to wish her a fatal outcome.

Finally I broke my rule and didn't ignore her. I couldn't help it. I yerfed, "Jump, fool cat!"

She just hung on, crying, "Help me!"

Michelle and Huey and Julian waved their arms and shouted.

"What? What?" said the man. He stopped sawing.

"Please, help our cat! Please rescue her!"

"Oh, it's a cat," the man said. "I thought it was a squirrel gone crazy."

He hung his saw over his shoulder and pulled Fiona's claws loose from the branch. She spat sawdust. Electric-saw whining sounds came from her belly. I was afraid those sounds were a new talent she had discovered and would keep.

The man climbed down the ladder, brushed sawdust off Fiona, and put her in Michelle's arms.

"Thank you," Michelle said.

"That's one fool cat," the man said.

"I'm afraid so," Michelle said. "Fiona, you're trembling, you're a nervous wreck!

We've all had enough excitement for one day!"

We turned round and headed for home. Our walk was over. The worst walk I'd ever had! We'd hardly got out of the back yard! I had seen nothing! I had smelled nothing!

A week went by. Every morning Fiona walked with us. Every morning there was some kind of problem on the walk. A cat emergency of some kind. A cat catastrophe. A cat cataclysm.

A big crow attacked her. She stepped on an anthill. She got her head stuck in a hole. She got lost in the park.

And I never got a decent walk, not one decent walk! At my age, a Dog needs at least one decent walk per day!

Ignoring Fiona was useless. One morning while she was removing my Nibbles from my bowl, I had a talk with her.

I didn't bring up the Nibbles first. I didn't

want her to know that her soaking them in water bothered me.

"Cats stay behind when Dogs take walks with their families," I said.

She said, "Dog, I am not just any Cat. I am *Fiona*. Fiona *never* stays behind."

She called herself by her own name. That confused me. It made me feel as if there were two Fionas – when one of her was more than enough.

"Fiona," I said, "at night, why do you get into the Blanket Cave with Huey and me, instead of sleeping in Julian's Blanket Cave?"

"Huey's is better. It's warmer, because there are two of you in it," she said.

"But he's *my* boy! That's *our* Blanket Cave!"

"It was."

"Why not be comfortable?" I coaxed. "Julian's Blanket Cave has much more space."

Fiona extended her ivory claws. She studied them in a leisurely way. "That's no problem, dog. When others are sleeping, I push. I always get all the space I want."

She yawned. Her breath carried traces of wild smells from our walks that I had never sensed at all because of being on a lead. They made me feel desperate. I had to know what I had missed.

"So what did you nose on our walks?" I asked her.

"Beetles, under a fallen log. Wild catnip – fabulous! An owl. Fish."

"What kind of fish?"

"By the lake. Rotting ones. It was more a stink than a smell."

She had smelled dead fish. And I hadn't even got close enough to sniff them! Truly, this is a world without justice!

"Dead fish!" I said. "My favourite! It's so good to roll in them, to wear dead fish perfume when you go hunting."

"I am a great hunter," she said. "A Balinese has no need for dead fish perfume." And she stuck her nose in the air.

I should have walked away. But her nose attracted me. I thought, If I touch her nose, I'll smell a little bit of all the things that she's smelled.

I had never wanted to touch noses with her before.

"May I touch noses with you?" I asked.

"If you wish," she answered, as if she were doing me a big favour.

Such a cool and tiny nose, but calm, not twitchy like the bunnies' noses.

Under the scent of soggy Nibbles, I smelled the tiniest but most awesome trace of dead fish perfume.

I couldn't stop myself. I thanked her.

"Dog, any time," she said.

"May I ask you another question?"

"Dog, you may."

"Fiona – I don't mean to criticize – but why do you always drink out of my water bowl instead of your water bowl?"

"Your water bowl is better."

"And why do you mush all my Nibbles into the water you paw out of my water bowl?"

"Nibbles taste better that way."

"Fiona — am I always going to have to share my Nibbles?"

She batted a wet Nibble across the floor.

"Yes."

She washed her paws in my water bowl and licked them dry.

"Please, Fiona," I said, "could you try to leave my water bowl alone?"

No answer. She cleaned her right ear with her right paw. She cleaned her left ear with her left paw, then started over cleaning her right ear again. I thought she had already finished with that one, but no.

That's how cats are. When it comes to ear polishing, they never finish.

"About your water bowl," she said. "Maybe I will drink other water. I don't promise I will. But I will think about it."

A Dog's Way

I have become a catologist – a student of cats. So far my studies are based on only one cat, Fiona. I think that is enough to draw certain conclusions. At least, for me it is. Maybe more than enough.

So far, I conclude this: a Dog's way is not a cat's way. A Dog's way is to be loyal, make promises, and keep them.

A cat's way is never to promise anything to anybody. A cat's way is to live continually considering and reconsidering its pleasures – so when it pounces on them, it never misses.

But Fiona had listened to one of my complaints, at least.

She still didn't drink from her water bowl, but she stopped drinking from mine. However, she still splashed water from my bowl onto the floor and dropped my Nibbles in the puddles.

I asked her why.

Fiona said, "It confuses the enemy."

I said, "Do you mean me?"

"No, dog," she said. "By putting your wet Nibbles on the floor, I am keeping wolves away. I am also keeping big Cats away. Panthers. *I* might get along with a panther, but *you* wouldn't like seeing them around here."

"I don't understand," I said.

"Dog, don't you know *anything*?" Fiona said. "Wet Nibbles on the floor scare panthers and wolves."

"Who told you that?"

"There are some things a Cat just knows."

She sat like a queen, looking like that huge riddle cat made of stone, the Great Sphinx, that I have heard is in a place called Egypt.

"Scaring panthers and wolves? I don't see how that works."

"Have you seen any panthers here? Have you seen any wolves?"

"No," I said, "but—"

"You see? It works. Or at least it's working so far, and I'm going to keep it up."

She continued to spill my water, but she didn't drink it. Instead, she drank from the saucers of the flowerpots. She drank from puddles in the park. She drank from the birdbath. For a long time that was it, as far as I knew.

One night I was sitting next to Huey

while he did his homework. Even though he didn't stroke me much, I was very happy. Fiona was not around, jumping up on his papers and curling her tail around his head the way she liked to do. It was just me and my boy together, the way it used to be.

Then I heard Fiona crying. She sounded far away.

I don't know what is the matter with me. With my mind. There I was, happy with my boy, and the next thing you know, I was trotting all over the house, looking for a cat that I was not missing *at all*.

A good Dog can't help being good. It's tragic.

I got to the White Pond Room, a room where Fiona likes to hang out. The Fiona noises were coming from it. The door to it was closed.

By accident, somebody in my family had shut her in the White Pond Room – a good place for her, I thought. The longer she stayed there, the longer I could be alone with my boy.

She heard the sound of my paws.

"Dog! Dog! Get me ow-ow-ow-ow OUT!" she said.

I yerfed to her. "Be calm. You like that room, so enjoy it a while."

"Dog! Get me ow-ow-ow-ow OUT!"

Maybe she was in trouble. I trotted back to the Boy Sleeping Room. I yerfed to get Huey to go to the White Pond Room with me.

He said, "Tiger, I'm busy. This work was due last week!"

I could still hear Fiona's cries. Desperate complaints were nothing new for her, but this time she sounded as if she meant it.

I yerfed again.

Huey said, "Tiger, don't be a pest!"

I hate whining. It hurts my throat. Nevertheless, I whined.

"Tiger! Are you sick? Go eat grass! Go drink water!" Huey said.

He didn't move an inch.

I had to get him to the White Pond Room. I took his pencil.

He chased me.

"Stop it, Tiger! Bad dog!" he shouted. "You could lose Hot Chilli Flavoured Tortilla Chips FOR GOOD!"

I didn't stop. I ran all the way to the White Pond Room and sat with my nose pointing at the door. There wasn't any noise from inside. I whined. I whined loudly.

Huey caught up with me. I dropped his pencil.

"At least you didn't break it," he said. "Back to work!"

"Dog! Dog! Get me ow-ow-ow-ow-ow OUT!" Fiona howled.

"Tiger, I get it now!" Huey opened the door to the White Pond Room. "Fiona! How uncool! You're in the toilet!"

She was in the deepest and steepest and slipperiest of the white ponds, with her fur soaking wet, her feet and claws slipping and sliding all over and never taking hold.

"I can't hold on! My legs are giving out! I'm going to drown!"

Huey lifted her out, all dripping.

"Dog!" she said. "I was on the edge of this pond — drinking from it. And then I slipped and fell! And this white pond is so hard I couldn't get my claws into it! I couldn't climb out! It's pretty and smells good, but the shores of it are so horrible and hard!"

"Are you ever a yowler!" Huey said.

He wrapped her in a towel.

"Julian," he called, "Fiona got into trouble!"

Julian came running. He and Huey washed Fiona with soap in the biggest white pond, even though Fiona insisted, in her very loudest voice, that she didn't want a bath.

"Why are you doing this? Why are you doing this? Why are you doing this?" she yowled.

They didn't answer, just kept rubbing her fur the wrong way till it stood up stiff and angry all over.

"Dog, why are they doing this to me?" she cried.

"I don't know why, Fiona, when you already washed in the other white pond."

Julian and Huey rinsed Fiona in fresh water. I talked to her.

"Fiona, about the other white pond, the one they call the toilet. Anyone could see how slippery and hard the shores are, so why did you go in?"

"You didn't want me to drink your water. Compared to flowerpot water and birdbath water, the white pond water smelled better. Anyhow, I am not anyone, I am Fiona. What anyone could see, I don't. I see other things. My special things to see."

What can you do with a cat like that who has to do everything her own way? Who puts your Nibbles in water on the floor? Who destroys the peace of your home? Who sleeps next to your boy even though you don't want her to?

Send her back to the Animal Shelter Hotel, I thought. She looked all wet and shivery and skinny, too – just the kind of cat that belongs in the Animal Shelter

Hotel. But somehow I couldn't say that to her.

"I was the one who found you. I was the one who heard you crying," I said.

"Thank you, dog," she said. "Of course, I would have been fine eventually. But you were very kind."

Julian and Huey got a fresh towel and dried her until her fur was soft and fluffy.

She walked over to me. I sniffed her. She had a sweet soap smell.

What a pity!

I took a deeper sniff, trying to recover even a hint of her dead fish fragrance — but besides the soap, all my nose could find in the chilly breath of her fur was Essence of Fiona — the sparkly, spangly, silly scent of Foolish.

I Learn That I Am Irish

There are many smells in the Bates house.

The best come from the Eating Room. The best of all is Hot Chilli Flavoured Tortilla Chips.

The worst and most scary smell is also in the Eating Room – down low, close to my nose. It comes from what they call the refrigerator – the part at the bottom, where there is a special drawer they call the freezer.

When I'm in the Eating Room, I avoid that drawer. I stay as far away from it as possible. Even when it's not open I nose its terrifying smell – the smell of Nothing.

It's not because I am silly or a coward that I fear and hate that smell. It is because of history.

Long, long ago, we Dogs and our Humans crossed a frozen sea to a great Emptyland. We went far, far north, to where snow put out the stars, so that day and night we could see nothing but snow falling from the sky landing and icing everything around us. Our Dog noses burned from cold and our breath froze in our throats. Every day we could smell less and less, until at last we smelled for the first time the terrible smell of Nothing. It terrified us.

Even those of us who were sometimes afraid of our Humans got close to them, close as skin to fur.

Our Humans breathed into our mouths; we breathed into our Humans' mouths. Humans and Dogs warmed each other and both lived. Then some curious Dogs went exploring and got lost from our Humans and died alone in the snow. Alone in the snow, smelling Nothing.

No Dog should die that way.

Ever since then, we Dogs have known that we must never leave our Humans. That's what the spirits of the ancestors tell us, their spirits that speak in our hearts, in our blood.

They tell us another thing, too: If you want to live, stay away from the smell of Nothing.

In the Bates Eating Room, when someone opened the freezer drawer, I could see inside to crystals of white ice and shapeless odourless dead stuff, and the deadly No-Smell whirled out like frozen white smoke burning, and my nose knew nothing, and I couldn't even look any more. I was very scared.

If I were strong enough, I thought, I

would drag the freezer drawer out of the refrigerator and out of the Bates home and never, ever, let it come back.

One day Fiona crawled into the back of a drawer in the Family Lie-Around Room. Somebody shut the drawer and she was trapped, until Michelle heard her and let her out.

She came out switching her tail indignantly. "Who trapped me?" she demanded.

"Nobody," I said. "You trapped yourself! If you don't want to be a prisoner, stay out of drawers! Going into drawers is a mistake."

It was a mistake to suggest that she had made a mistake.

She settled down on the couch. "No Cat has ever been attacked by a panther or a wolf in a drawer," she said. "Drawers are safe places."

"But there are no wolves or panthers around here!" I said.

"They don't come to where Cats spend a lot of time in drawers," Fiona said. "I go into drawers so they won't come. And they don't. You should thank me. Compared to a wolf or a panther, you are not all that big yourself, you know."

"I am not big, but I *reflect*, and that is my power," I said.

"Dog, you live your way," she said. "But as for me, if I ever think of wolves or panthers, I will look for a drawer to think in."

A few nights later, I was reflecting and dozing on the floor of the Family Lie-Around Room. Fiona was nearby, polishing her ears.

I fell asleep. When I woke, she was gone.

Usually when I didn't see her, I could catch a tiny fresh smell of Foolish and know at once where she was.

This time, there was no fresh smell of Foolish.

I got up. I tossed my head so my eardrums would be uncovered and I could hear better. But I didn't hear her anywhere.

I trotted all over the house, using all my olfactory capacity. I nosed around outside. Nowhere was there any fresh Fiona smell of Foolish.

I felt dread – the same dread of No-Smell the ancestors must have felt as they crossed the burning cold Emptyland.

And that dread made me think: Could it be that Fiona had got into the No-Smell freezer drawer? Was that why she had no smell any more?

I went to the Eating Room and sat in front of the refrigerator, closer than I had ever been to it, and pointed my nose at the freezer drawer, and yerfed and yerfed to my family, louder than I'd ever yerfed.

They came running.

"I was afraid it was a burglar. No

burglar," Ralph said.

Michelle looked at my food bowl. "You still have your Nibbles, Tiger!" she said. "So what's your problem?"

I yerfed again.

"Pesky dog! *Bad dog!* Stop it, Tiger!" Ralph said.

I yerfed louder. I yerfed faster.

Ralph put his hand on my head and pushed me towards the floor. That was an instruction – a humiliating instruction – to stop yerfing.

My head was pressed against the linoleum, which I have never enjoyed. If I just stopped yerfing, Ralph would say, "Good dog, Tiger!"

But if I stopped, maybe Foolish Fiona would die.

I kept yerfing.

Ralph lifted his hand and let my head go. He sighed. "What a racket! I hate to say this, Tiger, but you're behaving badly. A nice, quiet, pedigree cat is so much less trouble than you!"

Ralph had just said two unjust, untrue things, but did I even turn to look at him? No. I kept on yerfing. And finally, I did the most painful deed I have ever done – I reached out to touch the horrible disgusting No-Smell freezer drawer with my nose.

Ralph took hold of my collar. "Out to the rabbit hutch!"

"Dad, wait a minute!" Huey said. "Don't make him go! He's not just yerfing. I think he's telling us something!"

Ralph freed my head.

I stopped yerfing. I kept my nose pointed straight ahead.

"He's pointing, see!" Huey said. "Pointing like a hunting dog. Right in front of our noses! He's pointing at the freezer!"

"Let's see," Ralph said. He pulled the

freezer drawer open.

Burning white No-Smell smoke rolled out of it. Ralph bent down and reached to the back of it and brought out Fiona — motionless and stiff and all covered in No-Smell, as if she was No-Cat, no cat at all.

"No!" everybody said. "Oh no!"

Fiona's deadly No-Smell went right through me, into my bones. I didn't want to touch her, but I was filled with pity. I licked her cold body, licked ice crystals off her fur and her whiskers, so that even if she was dying, she wouldn't die without a smell. Because any animal, even a dying cat, should have a smell, because without a smell there is no meaning and without a meaning there is no life.

It was the bravest thing I had ever done.

But she didn't move.

Ralph stroked the places where I had licked Fiona. "It's worth a try," he said.

"You've got the right idea, Tiger, it's just that your tongue's not big enough."

He began to rub Fiona's body all over. When his hands got too cold, Michelle rubbed her. Then Julian. Then Huey.

And Fiona stirred at last. She woke. She raised her head. She talked in a dazed way. Not to anybody else. To me.

"Dog," she said. "There was so much darkness! Where were you?"

"I was right here," I said. "I was right

here almost all the time."

"Dog, you don't know how it is inside there! When they open it, it is very light and chilling bright, but when they close it, it is blinding dark. Too dark! I jumped in fast when Michelle put some sweet fish sticks in – but once I was in, I couldn't smell or taste or eat! Not fish sticks, not anything!

"Dog, tell me! Have I lost a lot of hair? I know I lost some! It stuck to the ice in there. There were icicles in my tongue. My eyes were starting to freeze and the burning cold dark shot all through me! It's not good in there! Don't ever go in there, dog!"

As if I ever would.

"She's weak, but she's meowing! She's going to live!" Ralph said.

"Fiona, Tiger saved you!" Huey said.

"I yerfed and pointed at the freezer so they would open it," I told her. "I yerfed even though Ralph called me pesky."

"Dog, you are not pesky! You are great!" Fiona said. "I thank you with all my heart, Tiger! You are more than a Dog! You are a Friend!"

We all sat in the Eating Room. Fiona lay in Michelle's lap, wrapped in a blanket. I pressed against the blanket to keep Fiona warm.

"It was amazing the way Tiger pointed," Ralph said. "Maybe he's part Irish setter."

"He could be part Saint Bernard, too," Michelle said, "making such a daring rescue of a fellow creature from freezing cold."

I'm a saint, and I'm Irish! I thought. I didn't know exactly what that meant, but it sounded good.

Julian gave Fiona warm milk to drink. Huey gave me fresh, crisp Nibbles, the kind I hardly ever get any more, and heaps of Hot Chilli Flavoured Tortilla Chips.

"It doesn't matter what breed he is,"

Huey said. "He's a rescue dog!"

A rescue Dog! I could feel it inside me – not just the word, but the meaning of it. I never knew what I was before. I knew I was a Dog, which is the most important thing, sure. But I didn't know what kind.

It didn't matter if no one could say what kind of Dog I had been born, or that I didn't have papers like Fiona. What mattered was something else completely.

A Dog needs a job, a purpose, something to accomplish with his life. I was a middle-aged Dog, a dignified Dog, rich in experience, yet I hadn't known any special purpose. I could have looked for a special purpose for ever and never found it. But through Fiona, my purpose found me.

Who would think a simple cat that smelled of Foolish could teach an experienced Dog – a dignified, reflective Dog – a big, important thing like that?

The Joining

Through the open windows of the Family Lie-Around Room, green-cut-grass and oily-lawn-mower smells blew in. Fiona and I both wanted to go outside, but Huey told us we couldn't. We were working. So was he. He was an artist, and we were his models.

He was making a birthday present for Ralph – a colour portrait of Fiona and me. He couldn't draw us outside, he said, because outside we would move around too much. He wanted us to be still.

I sat in Ralph's big chair with my ears

flopped down, very bored. Fiona sat on top of the couch in a glow of sunshine, purring.

"The sun admires me," she said. "In a previous life, Tiger, I was a professional model."

"How do you know you even had a previous life?" I asked.

"Cats always have nine lives," she said. "Everybody knows that."

Dogs deserve even more, I thought, but who knows if we'll get them?

Huey had a pencil, a rubber, markers, and an extra-big piece of paper. He drew and rubbed out, drew and rubbed out, and finally painted on the paper with the markers.

When he was done he blew on his picture and showed it to Fiona and me.

He had drawn us touching noses.

"Looks just like me!" Fiona said. "Only a little less beautiful."

Well, yes, I thought, any Human can draw a cat. I have seen those drawings chalked on pavements many times. To draw a cat, it only takes a few circles, a couple of lines for whiskers, and you're done. Nothing really to look at afterwards, either. But Dogs — our shapes are more interesting, more difficult.

For certain, it had taken Huey more time to draw me.

"Tiger, you look a little bit like a goat," Fiona said. "In the picture, I mean."

"It's all right," I said. I was pleased with Huey's picture. I've always wanted to have longer legs. In Huey's portrait, I had them.

Huey had given me a very long neck, too,

a bit like the neck of a giraffe, so my nose could reach way down and touch Fiona's. I didn't mind that either. That detail reminded me how much taller I am than she is.

"You don't really look like you," Fiona said.

I explained to her. "An artist sees in a special way, Fiona. Like you. There's more than one way for things to be true."

"But my way is better," Fiona said.

"That's what we all think," I told her.

"Good! I'm glad everyone thinks my way is better!" she said.

"That's not what I meant," I said.

"Everything's clear and we can go now," Fiona said.

Huey put his picture between the pages of a magazine and let us outside. Just for fun, I chased Fiona up a tree. Just for fun, she pretended to be scared of me.

She stopped partway up the trunk. "The

sun worships me," she said. "It wants me closer. It begged me to climb higher — but I said no."

Aha! She hadn't climbed high the way she used to! She isn't so foolish any more, I thought. She was older and wiser, which was a good thing. But it made me sad, too. If she should ever lose her spangly, silly smell of Foolish, I knew I'd miss it very much.

Through the open windows of the Boy Sleeping Room, a green-grass smell washed in, damp and full of night.

Julian was showing Huey his present for Ralph — a paper with some little flowers and cars drawn around the border and no Dogs or cats at all.

"See, Huey!" Julian said. "See how I put the words *Happy Birthday Gift Certificate* at the top. That makes it sound very official! I've written on it: *Dad — the garbage will be professionally carried out to the street for you once a week for one year.* And underneath I've signed it with my name."

"Cool," Huey said. "Do you want to see what I made?"

Gently he took his portrait out of the magazine.

Julian considered it. He breathed heavily. He ran his hand over the top of his head. Julian does that when he's brushing worries away.

"So what do you think?" Huey said.

"Well . . ." Julian said.

"Well what?" Huey said.

Julian sighed a deep sigh. "You know, Huey, it's nice. Only it doesn't look too much like *them*.

"What you could do, Huey, is this. Tomorrow in the morning there would be time for you to make a gift certificate like mine. You could officially promise to sweep the garage every week."

"And not give Dad my portrait?"

"Well, you could give that to him, too, of course, but maybe also something else would be even better."

Julian got out a book about Dogs and cats and opened it. "See, Huey. Dogs and cats don't look exactly the way you have them looking."

He showed Huey all the things that were wrong with his portrait.

Huey looked from the book to his picture, and from his picture to the book, seeing all the things that were wrong.

There were things wrong with his portrait, for sure.

But the things Julian missed seeing were the things that were right. For instance, the noses were exactly right. Also the tails. Also the friendship, the new friendship between me and Fiona. Even if I did look a little like a goat, and Fiona a little like a snowman, still you could see the friendship between us.

That is important. It's a big talent for a Human to be able to make a drawing showing something invisible — something valuable. Lots of Humans can draw Dogs and cats, but not that many can draw friendship, and friendship is a beautiful thing.

I told Huey, "Your drawing is good."

Once again the tragedy of our not having a common language came between us. All he understood was "Yerf!"

"Quiet, Tiger!" he said. He wiped his eyes with the back of his hand, as if too much staring at his portrait had made them very tired.

"I guess it's not so good. Not good like I thought." He stuck his portrait back into the magazine he had taken it out of and dropped the magazine into the waste-paper basket.

He didn't say if he would make a gift certificate in the morning. He didn't say anything more at all.

He got into our Blanket Cave alone and very fast, without taking off any of his clothes or even his shoes.

He pulled the blankets over his head. I heard him make one little whimpering sound.

Fiona glanced at our Blanket Cave. "Sadness has never appealed to me," she said. "I will sleep elsewhere."

"My place is with my boy," I said.

I jumped onto our Blanket Cave. Huey felt my weight and let me into it and took off his shoes and knocked them out onto the floor without ever showing his face outside our cave. I licked Huey's hands, then his face. On sad nights, a good Dog will never leave his boy's face unlicked.

Huey made tiny snuffling noises. I stuck my nose against his ear and snuggled close to him. He lay between my front paws and hugged me, and that's the way we fell asleep.

I dreamed of my ancestors. In the dream they were very tall, and glowing. I asked them if they would let my boy share my dream. They said, "Do you want a dream of Joining?" and I answered, "Yes, that's what I want."

"Young pup," they said, "we will grant your wish. You and your boy will have this dream. It will make you two special beings – Dream Keepers."

My dream became so clear, and I remember it so well, that when I think of it, it's as if it's still happening:

I take Huey's hand in my mouth, very gently, and run with him a long way through the night. Together we come to a great swamp where old leaves, dying, fall into great pools of still water. I smell a delicious smell of decay. I remember the secret smell of Ralph, and I know that this is the swamp Ralph's own dog took him to when he was a boy, the swamp of the rich smells that became part of Ralph.

This is the swamp of the great Joining. I know this, because I can feel Huey and me becoming one. Our noses become one nose. He becomes partly Dog, and I become partly boy. I feel many strange changes in myself. I even start to understand what drawing is, as if I were an artist like Huey.

We stand together in the great swamp where time dissolves, where dreams and creations are born, where today decaying becomes the food for tomorrow. I think of Fiona. Was there ever a time when I didn't love her? It seems as if there never was.

The ancestors speak once more. "Dream Keeper, dream deeper," they say.

Huey begins to dream, too. Because we dream together with one heart, whatever we need to do, we can do.

We explore the swamp, which leads to a river. We enter the river and, among pink dolphins and huge fish of many colours, we swim to the sea. We live among strange creatures at the bottom of the sea, then rise again to where the moon glitters on the water, and the moon lifts us and holds us in its arms.

It's many Dog hours or maybe years before the moon returns us to the green swamp and then back at last to the best place of all, our Blanket Cave.

In the morning, waking, I put my paws around Huey. He puts his arms around me. I wonder how his feet feel. My paws feel strange, a little sore, as if I'd been running all night, and they have a strange, rich smell that I like but have never smelled before. A special smell of green.

My boy whispers in my ear. "I had a strange dream about you, Tiger, something about a swamp, only there was more, much more, but I can't remember all of it, only that it felt really good the way we were together."

We stay close until even inside our Blanket Cave there's light, and we know it's time to open it to the world. The sun has risen. Julian is standing by us.

"Huey, Dad's awake! We should give him our presents right away," he says. "I got this paper for you, so you can make a gift certificate like mine."

Huey reaches out a hand. He pulls the magazine with his portrait out of the waste-paper basket. He takes the portrait out of the magazine and holds it carefully.

"Thanks, Julian," he says, "but I'm not making any certificate. I like my picture. You don't have to like it, but I think it's good. I'm giving it to Dad."

He sets his feet down firmly on the floor and takes a deep breath. His Huey nose is more sensitive now, being part Dog nose. I see that he has special feet, too – feet like his dad's – strong feet for taking a stand, quick feet for going where he'll need to go. Feet with a bit of swamp fragrance to them.

The sun comes in the window with rays that make rainbows in my eyes. My eyes blink shut and open with a deeper sight.

For one brief instant I see the far, far future – my boy an old man, still searching out and finding his right path, as I, long gone from this world, return to visit him in dreams.